INTO THE FOURTH DIMENSION

INTO THE FOURTH DIMENSION

BY

A. C. HANLON

1977

THE THEOSOPHICAL PUBLISHING HOUSE

ADYAR, MADRAS 600020, INDIA

68, Great Russell Street, London, WCIB 3BU, England

Post Box 270, Wheaton, Illinois 60187, U.S.A.

ISBN   0-8356-7529-7

PRINTED IN INDIA

At the Vasanta Press,
The Theosophical Society, Adyar, Madras 600020

CONTENTS

PREFACE

THE contents of this book consist largely of about a dozen articles, or extracts from them, that have been published in "The Theosophist" and "Theosophy in New Zealand". The first article appeared in the New Zealand magazine, May 1919, and the second in "The Theosophist" March 1922, and the last in the latter magazine, March 1968. Some of the "Sonnets of Space and Time" were published in "The Auckland Star" 1930 to 1933, and two in "Contemporary Poets 1974" by the Regency Press, London.

The famous British mathematician, Bertrand Russell once wrote:— "Mathematics rightly viewed possesses supreme beauty—a beauty cold and austere, like that of sculpture. The true spirit of delight, the exaltation, the sense of being more than man, which is the touchstone of the highest excellence, is to be found in mathematics as surely as in poetry."

This exaltation will surely come to those who succeed in visualizing a four-dimensional figure for, in this act, there is not merely the creation of a figure in four dimensions, but the experiencing of a power, a spatial power, not to be known while we are limited to a space of three dimensions. It is probable that the creative power of genius in art, music, literature, and in other fields of original activity, derives its inspiration from higher-dimensional space.

To visualize the simplest four-dimensional form is to experience something of this power for, by this act, we have taken the first step " Into the Fourth Dimension ".

CHAPTER ONE

SPACE IS MY ADVENTURE

How did my adventure begin? When was my first experience of space? I remember at the age of four or five years while living in the gold-mining town of Waihi, awakening in panic from dreams of falling or nearly falling, down gaps or wells in the surface of a large gloomy plain over which I had been chased by enormous animals that, much later in life I was to discover, closely resembled the pre-historic dinosaur and pterodactyl, and similar creatures. The space I then experienced was not only the bottom-less emptiness into which, again and again, I was to fall, to be saved generally by awakening, but the space of time also for, in my dreams, I must have gone back a million years or more along the co-ordinate of time, a co-ordinate which, again years later, I

was also to discover was only a space co-
ordinate experienced as a succession of
' nows '.   At that early age however, I was
incapable of any speculation on my dreams;
all I felt was the terror.

It was about this time, though, that I had
my first objective experience of space.   A
telescope had been erected in the main street
of Waihi, and passers-by were invited to
gaze at the moon and stars for a payment
of a small coin.   This street, at the beginning
of this century, was very dusty but nevertheless
my first views of the stellar universe probably
stirred in me, however faintly, an interest
in the problem of the nature, not so much
of the planets, stars, and other heavenly
bodies, but rather of that medium in which
they all exist—space.   Or perhaps it was not
until a few years later in 1910, as I watched
Halley's Comet, stretched across most of the
Auckland sky, that I first began to feel the
fascination of that apparently infinite void
in which not only the myriad heavenly bodies
moved but of which man himself, in some
mysterious way, was part.   At that early age,
nine years, although it is unlikely I might

have begun to sense the possible truth that the life animating all living creatures is inseparable from that universal essence which we call space and which, while itself neither form nor matter, is basic to the existence of both. Perhaps another name for the life of the universe could be Absolute Space.

The next event to increase my awareness of space occurred about three years after the appearance of the comet. In the middle of the night I awakened to find within myself such a powerful sense of my own bodyless individuality, of my separate existence as the " I am " that I began to think of the many human beings living in all the other lands on the surface of this globe, and then to question why I should be in this particular body and not in one of the other members of this human race. As my mind went over the surface of the earth I felt the life which was my real self was the life in all other human beings. The mystery to be solved was why I apparently manifested or lived in one body and why it should be in this particular one. Perhaps I felt it had to be either all bodies or none. Later I was to hear of the process of re-incarnation, but this conception did not solve the mystery. It only substituted a line of bodies for a single one, and the problem remained.

A few years later, when I was seventeen, I was scanning the titles of books in a private library when one title held my attention. It was 'The Fourth Dimension' by C. Howard Hinton, M.A. Unaware of the meaning of the title I nevertheless took the book home to study. Until then my knowledge of geometry had been applied only to technical and practical purposes, but now geometry began to take on a significance and relationship to fundamental problems, such as the nature of consciousness, that compelled me to deeper study. It was then I began to consider the possibility of a dimension extra to the three dimensions of our physical and normal experience despite Hinton's own statement: "All attempts to visualize a fourth dimension are futile. It must be connected with a time experience in three-dimensional space." Some years later I was to come across an almost identical assertion by another writer on this subject,

P.D. Ouspensky, well known for his ' Tertium Organum ' and ' A New Model of the Universe '. In the latter book he wrote " The fourth dimension is unknowable." I was never to take either of these assertions on the impossibility of the experiencing of the fourth dimension seriously; indeed I came across them too late, for by then I had already seen in my mind a complete four-dimensional shape, the tesseract, whose three-dimensional sections were the limits of Hinton's research. Despite his repudiation of the possibility of the human mind seeing a four-dimensional shape, it was Hinton who brought me to that experience. At the age of seventeen then, just as the tones of an instrument, of the human voice, or hidden music, awakens a young musician to a realisation of his true vocation, so the simple phrase ' the fourth dimension ' made such an impact on my mind that I set out to discover what it really meant. I was soon to learn that no great knowledge of geometry is required for the visualization of four-dimensional forms, only a space sense developed to the point where it can conceive four co-ordinates or straight lines meeting in a common point, each pointing in a direction at right angles to the other three lines. Hinton, although he profusely illustrated his arguments with diagrams, never gave a complete drawing of a four-dimensional figure. The task I set myself was not to visualize such a figure as Hinton insisted it only could be visualized, that is as three-dimensional sections in succession but to conceive in one moment the complete four-dimensional shape. I recall how, night after night, I tried to bring the simple cubic boundaries of a four-dimensional form into such relationship with each other that they would be seen in the mind as the boundaries of an authentic four-dimensional shape, and higher space be fully experienced in a moment of time, if not sustained for a longer period.

The tesseract, then, was the shape I first worked with, largely because Hinton concerned himself mostly with cubes, and the tesseract is the equivalent in four-dimensional space, to the cube in three dimensional space. While concentrating on the task of visualizing or trying to visualize, this shape I never quite met with success. Sometimes I would be aware of bright lights and colours flashing about me, and strange warm or electric pressures especially on the top of my head, but at that stage I never managed to stabilise the complete four-dimensional form in my mind. When it seemed that all the eight cubes bounding the tesseract were about to settle into their correct relationship in four co-ordinates, and crown my efforts with success, something prevented the attainment of my goal. I never considered this frustration was because I was engaged on an impossible and hopeless undertaking, for in my mind there were premonitions of success, stimulated by partial glimpses or sensing of an known factor or power that almost took possession of the form I was trying to visualize but never quite succeeding. Years later I recalled these frustrations when concluding a sonnet on Herschel and his search for Uranus:

" So I, too, lost in midnight contemplation
 Have sought to pierce the age-old mystery
 Of time and space, and felt myself upon
 The brink of some transcendent revelation
 When lo ! intrudes one bright irrelevancy,
 And those immortal whisperings are gone."

One day however, after a period of little progress in my attempts at visualizing, while out walking and therefore mentally relaxed, the complete tesseract, in all its fullness, presented itself to my mind. As a result of this experience I wrote my first article describing, not merely the geometrical details of this four-dimensional ' cube ' which Hinton, and probably other writers unknown to me, had already logically deduced, but the method by which the figure could be truly visualized. Hinton, by denying the possibility of experiencing the fourth dimension in its fullness, denied himself the final experience and the devising of a sound technique for successful visualization.

Basically, then, the method I had adopted for visualizing four-dimensional forms was first of all to picture mentally in three dimensions all the components of the higher-dimensional shape, just as a drawing of a cube on a plane surface depicts all its individual parts but not its three-dimensional content; the next step was to make these components, lines, squares, and cubes, in the case of the tesseract take up their final position as

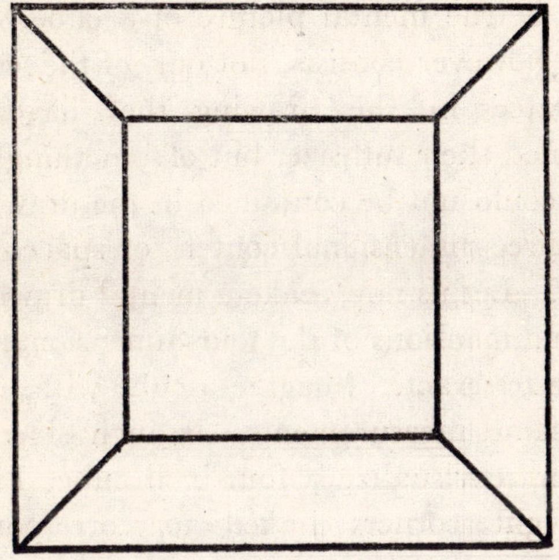

Fig. 1

boundaries of the four dimensional shape. In a drawing of a cube (Fig. 1) we have first the square, the sides say 6 inches long, then centrally within it another square, say 4 inch sides parallel to the larger square. Connecting the corresponding four corners of the two squares are four straight lines. The drawing is for all practical purposes two-dimensional. If now we mentally draw a small square perpendicularly away from the larger square, at the same time expanding it to the same size, and for a distance of six inches, we will have a true mental picture of a cube. This cube however consists, not only of the sections indicated in the drawing that have now assumed their full size, but of something extra that could not be contained in the drawing— the three-dimensional content or space of the cube. Let us now make a mental drawing in three dimensions of the four-dimensional cube —the tesseract. Imagine a cube with, to use the same measurements, six inch sides. In its centre visualize a four-inch cube (Fig. 2) its eight corners linked to corresponding

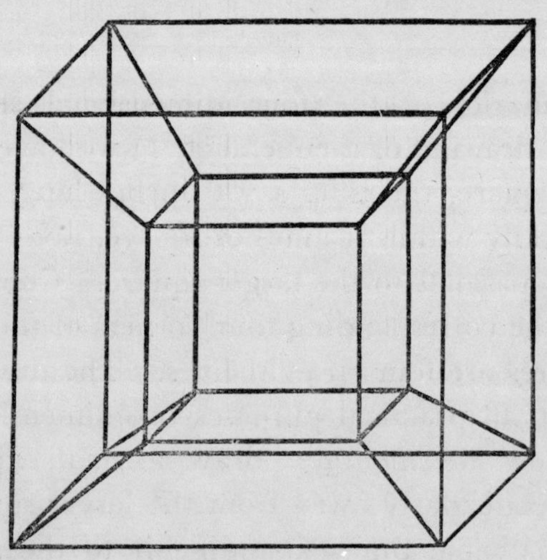

FIG. 2

corners of the larger cube by eight straight lines. We could make a model of this, in metal or wood. This model could be considered as a drawing in three dimensions of a four dimensional form and, just as on paper we cannot create the cube's spatial content, so this three-dimensional model cannot contain the four-dimensional space of the tesseract. To produce the four-dimensional shape we have to do precisely what we did in visualizing the cube. We have to move the small cube perpendicularly out of the larger one without moving it in the space of the larger cube.

When creating the cube by the perpendicular expanding movement, no movement whatsoever occurs in the six inch square and all four connecting lines grow evenly to their correct length when the visualizing process as already described is carried out. Similarly with the visualizing of the tesseract the small cube moves completely out of the larger cube from the moment the movement commences, and the six truncated pyramids assume their true cubic shape as the moving cube expands to the size of the larger cube. We then have a four-dimensional form bounded by eight equal cubes, and having a spatial quality impossible of expression in the mental three-dimensional picture or model, or in three-dimensional space. This, then was the procedure I developed for visualizing four-dimensional forms.

CHAPTER TWO

SPACE AND TIME

NEARLY sixty years ago, convinced of the reality of four-dimensional space in the only sense that it can be real, that is of a space in which forms require four co-ordinates for their complete definition as geometric structures I wrote my first article, describing a four-dimensional figure and how to visualize it. The question that might be asked of me now is, do I still believe that fourth dimension to be a fact? The answer today, as it would have been then, is—I believe in nothing. There is only one thing to do about facts, know them, not believe in them. No matter how logical, how beautiful, how convincing, certain ideas are, they must not become beliefs or their likely fate is to remain beliefs. The only thing is to know, and the first step toward knowledge is to have no beliefs.

I know there is one world, one universe. I do not believe in the fourth dimension, nor in three dimensions but I know both to be contained in absolute space. There are some who say the fourth dimension does not exist as though they know, or the authority they believe in knows of this non-existence. I myself have always found it hard enough to know what exists without asserting what does not exist.

Right from the beginning I considered four-dimensional shapes possible, and that it was also possible and therefore natural for the mind to conceive these forms. In my early studies I found most works on this subject, principally Hinton's and Ouspensky's, too involved or too theoretical. Nevertheless it was, while studying the former writer's coloured sections of a tesseract, that I had my first vision of it. It was clear to me then that the fundamental or 'Platonic' four-dimensional shapes are so simple that an equally simple technique for visualizing them could be devised.

Without concerning oneself at the outset with any particular four-dimensional shape, the first necessity is to understand what space is, the pure existence in which occurs the forms and motions of limited existence. The limited condition we are familiar with is a three-dimensional one. Our first task is to understand why it is three-dimensional, to see that this limitation is of matter, but not of space itself, for space is that in which all possible events happen.

The geometrical details of four-dimensional shapes are comparatively easy to understand. The difficulty is to unite them so that they become a container of a higher space. In order to visualize a four-dimensional shape we have to develop what Krishnamurti calls 'pure awareness'. As long as we cling to jealously, greed, hate, we cannot know love, and so long as we cling to our three-dimensional limitations, so long as we do not regard them squarely without reaction, we will not know that reality which is pure space, and in which higher dimensional shapes naturally appear. The process of visualizing these forms, which cannot exist in a three-dimensional space or consciousness, is indeed an art for, just as the intuition of beauty in the artist makes a painting a work of art, so the intuition of space in the thinker makes possible the creation of a higher-dimensional form. Creative energies of a high order are at work in the souls of both.

If the universe, if mind, if consciousness, if all existence, was fixed in three dimensions no intuition of a higher dimensional order could ever enter human consciousness; no urge to even understand the limitations of physical existence would be felt, for there would be no real higher existence to originate and give substance to such an intuition or urge. As art derives its secret power from a sublime source so research into the fourth dimension has its inspiration in the tangible reality of the four-dimensional world itself.

The problem of time and space has been a favourite subject with thinkers from days immemorial, for it arises naturally in the mind as it contemplates the external world of matter and motion. Thus it arose in my mind, first as an intellectual problem, and then as a challenge to my whole being. I found that no real step in understanding the nature of time and space could be taken without voyaging, on the one hand, into uncharted regions of space and, on the other, into the mysterious depths of my own nature. In other words, space was not only basic to the universe, it was equally a necessary condition of my own existence as a conscious being. At times it seems there is no division or barrier between the space in which the stars move and myself as soul or spirit; and the Kantian doctrine of time and space as modes of the mind becomes a simple though powerful experience.

In this room, where I write, I am enclosed by the vertical planes of its walls and the horizontal planes of the floor and ceiling, making three sets or parallel planes, each set at the right angles to the other two; but though they enclose my body they do not restrict my mind, for my imagination extends beyond them to the external world, to the east and west, the north and south, and through the earth and overhead to the stars, in all directions. There in the vast abysses beyond this earth, beyond the orbits of Jupiter and Pluto revolving in the outer darkness of our planetary system, beyond the galaxies of myriad suns, out to the most distant spiral nebulae ever photographed, there, indeed, it seems, is ample space for the adventuring mind.

Yet not because my mind can voyage far beyond the walls of this room, and through contemplation of the firmament in some mysterious way become part of it, am I released from these confining planes. By that act of contemplation all I have done is to increase the size of my room. Its fundamental limitations remain the same, for the space of the stellar universe is precisely the same as the space of this room. The spatial structure of the room, however, is more obvious to the eye, and to the mind, for at each of the eight corners of a square room the three co-ordinates or dimensions are to be seen radiating from it in three distinct directions The position of any object in the room can be determined completely by reference to any set of three lines.

When we consider the space exterior to the room we find there are no visible co-ordinates we can relate the heavenly bodies and their movements to; it might be disputed therefore that the physical universe is three-dimensional. Astronomy here provides the proof by showing that all that is visible to normal sight is also visible through a telescope rigidly mounted to point only along the three co-ordinates, or into the space defined by them. It may be objected that no instrument can be fixed with regard to the stars since the earth is rotating on its axis while also moving round the sun, and all heavenly bodies, including the stars, are similarly in perpetual motion. This is true, but at any given moment (when the whole universe is still) the three co-ordinates define exactly the relative positions of all bodies in physical space.

The structure of the cosmos in the relativity continuum, however, does not consist only of heavenly bodies and their distribution in a space of three dimensions. The stars, clusters, and nebulae, are in continual motion and more fully to determine the phenomena we must take into account their relative velocities. We assume that bodies move in three-dimensional space, but they do not; they move in time, the fourth co-ordinate in the physical four-dimensional continuum. Since no motion takes place in three dimensions, and we are aware of motion, and change in three-dimensional relationships, then what we are experiencing is really a succession of three-dimensional universes distributed along the dimension of time. These universes are not isolated from one another but form a homogeneous entity whose structure, as a four-dimensional universe, could be visualized and experienced if we gave to time the so-called objectivity of space. We would then see the Einsteinian continuum as a timeless four-dimensional design in which the distinguishing shapes would not be globes, as in three-dimensional space, but spirals of globular cross-section interweaved throughout a four-dimensional space to form a pattern of mysterious beauty.

Here then, surely, is a space that must satisfy any mind, and give the final answer to the question—what is space? In a certain way infinitely greater than the universe of the telescope, and with an indescribable quality conferred on it by its extra dimension, this timeless universe must surely be the goal of my quest. Nevertheless, although I cannot sustain for long the vision of this four-dimensional universe, I know the answer is not there. Looking along the spiral that is the earth's track in ' past ' time for a number of coils, and following the thread of my own consciousness, I find myself a child again. Beyond that point I cannot press much further in consciousness without feeling myself withdrawing into unconsciousness.

It is, however, that break in consciousness which reveals to me that my adventure has only begun. Not that alone for answering to outer space is the spaciousness of an undying part of my own nature, and this quest must go on until I find a world that coincides at every point with my eternal self. There is a quality in the three-dimensional, as there is in the spiral universe, which evokes a response from me as a spirit, and that quality is the boundlessness of space within its three of four co-ordinates. If the experience of illimitable space is the object of my adventure then I must either, by a process that would appear endless, conquer each co-ordinate of space by adding dimension after dimension to my mind, or forsake the mental process and discover the essence of space in myself.

Because time and space are of the very fabric of the mind it is compelled to conceive the eternal in terms of separation and movement, the eternal as events in time and space. It cannot do otherwise and, as the unutterable mystery of creation presses more and more on the soul, the mind finds release by adding further dimensions to its powers of perception, by seeking larger horizons in the objective universe. Always will the astronomer hunger after that which lies beyond the most distant nebula he knows, beyond the known past and future, and always will he hunger so long as he lives in the mind's interpretation of reality. Only in the realization of the universe as Pure Being, and therefore untouched by the problem of beginning and end, as that in which clusters, stars, planets, human beings, and atoms are simultaneously and inseparably one, can we experience reality. This is the mystic astronomy beyond the understanding of the scientific astronomer, as such, needing neither instruments nor calculations, for the seer and seen are one in eternity. There no light of finite velocity carries its message across the immensities between lonely worlds, for Light Eternal illumines the spirit and makes it one with Eternal Being.

CHAPTER THREE

FIRST STEPS

In this chapter it is proposed to show how an understanding of the fourth dimension can be arrived at.   Perhaps one reason why the study of the Fourth Dimension is not attempted is because of a certain indefiniteness or intangibility that seems to surround it.   Also the subject from its outset is at once metaphysical, and apparently confusing in the labyrinths of mathematical reasoning through which this extra dimension has to be pursued. Yet it is not so confusing as it first appears, and persistence during the preliminary study will bring the student to the stage when the fascination of exploring higher space will be an incentive to still further effort.

The first stages, like the preliminaries of most subjects, present the greatest difficulties, perhaps because it is at the beginning that the foundations and fundamental principles are laid.   Also the introduction of a new line of thought makes a hitherto unknown demand upon the thinking faculties. An effort is required, at first, to make the mind occupy itself with a strange, and to the mind, heterodox thought; but when it has become accustomed to that thought the difficulty disappears. This is the case with the study of a higher space. The idea of extra dimensions to the three of physical space is so unusual to ordinary thought that some determination is required in laying the basis upon which the structure of higher knowledge will be surely built.

A conception of four-dimensional space can be gained by examining the conditions and relationships in one, two, and three dimensions, and observing carefully how analogous figures of these dimensions are linked together, and then by carrying the whole process a step further—into the fourth dimension—an understanding of this higher space can be arrived at.

One dimension we can represent by a straight line which has only one quality— length; that is its dimension. Now let us imagine a line-world as a straight line of indefinite length and think of beings living in this world. They would have bodies of one dimension, that is finite straight lines, the only forms possible in a line-world. It can be seen that growth can only be an increase in the length of the body. These creatures would be absolutely unconscious of any movement other than along this line, backward and forward. The idea of a direction extending away from their line of motion would be inconceivable to them, as inconceivable as, or more so than, the idea of a dimension extending away from our space is to us. Another strange thing is noticed about this one-dimensional world; a line being cannot pass another, and he must therefore have always the same two neighbours, although the distance between them can vary. To pass another a line-being must move completely out of this world; but this he cannot do since he is limited absolutely to the directions bounded for him by his neighbours.

One-dimensional space is a space in which movement is possible only in a line. A two-dimensional world is one in which movement is possible in two directions at right angles to each other—a plane surface.

We can imagine a plane-world as a vast flat surface upon which two-dimensional beings

live and move about. Movement is possible
to such beings anywhere on this superficies,
but in that direction which extends away from
it they cannot move nor, normally, understand
such a movement. The idea of a direction
lying away from their two-dimensional could
never, under ordinary circumstances, occur to
them; they only understand a back-ward and
forward, and left and right motion, and a
combination of these two movements. We can
imagine a plane-being as having a body
made of a very thin substance like a sheet of
paper, of the thickness of which he is unconscious. A two-dimensional being can
contact other beings and objects in his world
only by their edges, in the same way that we
three-dimensional beings can contact objects
in our world by their surfaces.

This being so, some curious facts about this
plane-world can be seen. If an inhabitant of
this world is surrounded by a line, for instance
a circle, then it will be completely imprisoned.
Escape would be impossible unless the line
was broken. A three-dimensional being could
not be caught by being surrounded by a line
in this manner since he could move out of the

circle in a direction extending away from the plane of the circle.

But this way of escape is not open to the plane-being for, of this direction that lies away from his world he has no conception or experience. His consciousness is limited to a plane and can only understand what takes place in that plane. Perhaps it would be better to say that a plane-being might understand something of a higher world, a three-dimensional one, but could not experience it.

The characteristic of this higher world is that in it there are three movements, each one at right angles to the other two, possible to a being of this world. Not only can we three-dimensional beings move backward and forward and left and right, but also up and down. By these three movements any point in our space can be reached as, in the case of a plane-being, any point in his space could be reached by two movements, left and right, up and down, assuming of course a circular world in which gravitation has its function. It is difficult for those with no conception of space, other than that of three dimensions, to imagine a space of two dimensions, in fact such a space seems an impossibility, since two-dimensionality appears to be only an abstraction. But two-dimensional conceptions, although abstractions to us, would be realities to a two-dimensional being.

As a line being can be imprisoned by points, and a plane being by lines, so can we be imprisoned by plane surfaces as, for instance the walls, floor and ceiling of a room. Following out the analogy of the two-dimensional prison and its inability to hold a three-dimensional being, we arrive at the conclusion that a three-dimensional prison cannot hold a four-dimensional being. This being can move in a direction to which we cannot point for, wherever we point the line of direction we indicate can only be in our space. This new direction extends completely out of our world, and nothing exists here but that it is open to the higher four-dimensional world. The fourth dimension expands from our world in the same way that the third dimension extends away from the plane world.

When the idea of what is meant by a dimension of space has been grasped then the student is ready for the higher dimension.

CHAPTER FOUR

VISUALIZING FOUR-DIMENSIONAL SHAPES

IT could be an axiom that the simplest things are the most difficult to understand. This is evident when we consider that philosophy, the highest expression of knowledge, is simplicity itself. The philosophic mind is the perfect mind because all personal attitudes have disappeared from it. Impersonality is the key-note of the philosopher; perhaps that is why philosophic truths are so difficult to grasp; not because the truths are so subtle but because one has to become, like them, impersonal. The process by which the mind is evolved from a material to a philosophic one is a purging process in which the personality is changed from the dominant to a subordinate position. And this purging process must be gone through to a certain extent before the mind can see the fourth dimension. The difficulty in seeing the fourth dimension is largely due to our self-centredness. The act of visualizing a higher figure is an act of self-realisation, of not only widening one's mental and material horizons, but of increasing the spaciousness of the soul. One naturally moves a step nearer to the heart of all things.

It should be obvious that any experiments intended to demonstrate the existence of a higher dimension cannot be undertaken in the usual way with physical materials and appliances, since the lesser cannot contain the greater. Three-dimensional instruments could not measure the minutest part of four-dimensional matter, for, in a special way, that small part is greater than the physical universe. A cube, no matter how small, is greater than a superficies of infinite extent. The experiment must of necessity be invisible to physical consciousness since its fulness cannot be rendered in terms of three-dimensional experience. The experiment must take place in the mind.

The following is a description of such an experiment, in which a figure corresponding in four dimensions to the tetrahedron is used. I have called it the super-tetrahedron. This figure is a four-dimensional " solid " enclosed by five tetrahedra, each tetrahedron contacting by means of its four triangular faces one face of each of the other four tetrahedra. This is not possible in three dimensions for, if one tetrahedron touch the other four in this manner, these four could not touch each other except at a line. The five tetrahedra related as first described are the outer boundaries of the four-dimensional figure. The appearance of the actual figure is hard to describe. It must be seen to be appreciated.

As a preliminary to the actual visualization, and as a stimulant to the imagination, the evolution that culminates in the super-tetrahedron can be mentally depicted. From the point evolves the line, then follows the equilateral triangle, and finally the tetrahedron. It is helpful, while picturing all this, to try to be the line, triangle, and tetrahedron, to feel their spatial limitations. This helps to clear the mind of space prejudices, and makes it receptive to the idea that space can be something different from that which it generally knows. There may be better ways of visualizing these higher figures than the methods I have used, but they are satisfactory so far as results are concerned.

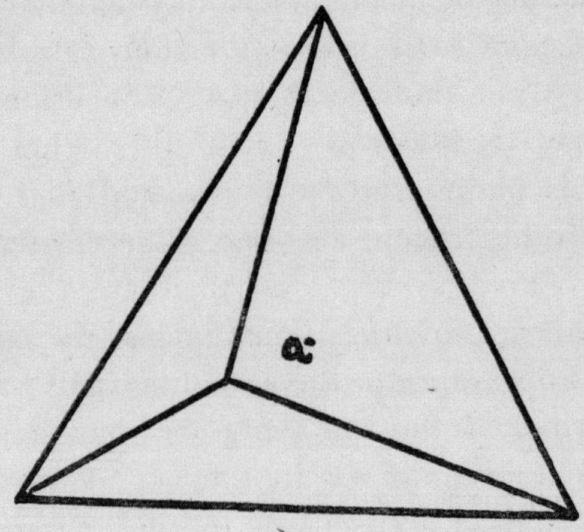

Fig. 3

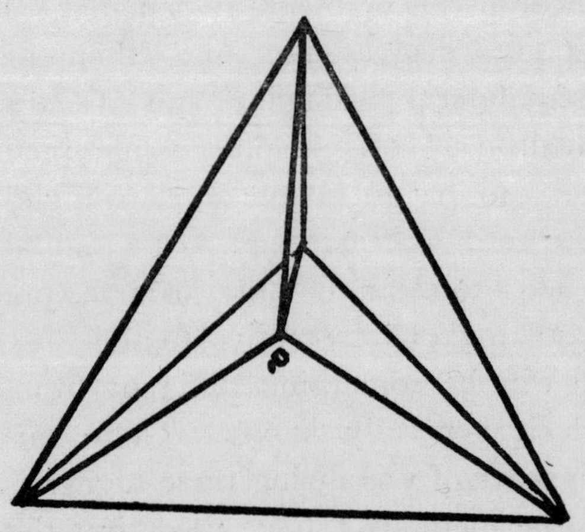

Fig. 4

First visualize a tetrahedron. Fig. 3; then from its centre " a " Fig. 4. extend a line to each of its corners. This will divide the volume, or shall we say " area " in anticipation, of the tetrahedron into four shortened tetrahedra. The whole figure, of course, is still three-dimensional. The reader must now try to look at the figure from four points of view at once, from the outside of each of the four triangles of the primary tetrahedron. This need not be done perfectly so long as it is done sufficiently well for the purpose, which is to keep a watch on all the exteriors of the tetrahedron at the one time. The next operation is to force the shortened tetrahedra to assume their true tetrahedral height, without shifting their bases, the four sides of the primary tetrahedron, and without entering into one another, and still meet in the point " a ". It seems a case of checkmate without a doubt. The conditions to be observed seem so rigid that no movement can take place. This feeling of rigidity is due to what could be called space prejudices. One of the results of visualizing higher-dimensional figures is the disappearance of spatial prejudices, and even personal ones. Geometry thus attains its full stature as a character builder, giving width and tolerance to the mind.

To make the four-dimensional form the four tetrahedra contained in the primary one have to go through this movement, and so nothing remains but to make them do it. The will must be constantly exerted in an endeavour to draw the centre or apex " a " away from the centre of the primary tetrahedron without moving it in the tetrahedron itself. It is a matter of the steady application of the will, at the same time feeling for the new direction, and then the "miracle" happens. The four tetrahedra previously contained in the primary one expand and there appears between the five tetrahedra a portion of four-dimensional space, the content of the super-tetrahedron. One is not confused by any intricacy in the construction of the figure for it is extremely simple. There can be no doubt as to the genuineness of the figure created. The authority of scientists or mathematicians who maintain that the fourth dimension is purely a mathematical quantity or conception gives way to the authority of experience.

All learnedness counts for nothing when a higher dimension has illumined the mind.

I have found an effective aid to visualizing four-dimensional figures is to attempt to understand a figure of a still higher dimension. The concentration developed in that exercise, when turned to the visualizing of a four-dimensional shape, makes that operation almost a form of relaxation. The simplest five-dimensional figure is an extension of the four-dimensional one we have just considered. From each of the five tetrahedral faces of the super-tetrahedron extends a super-tetrahedron into the fifth dimension, the five meeting in a common apex. The total six four-dimensional figures completely enclose a portion of five-dimensional space, the analogue of the tetrahedron in five dimensions. It is well to work out these figures for oneself. There is nothing arbitrary about them for they can be built up logically. The simplest form, for example, in any dimension is enclosed by one more side than its dimensions. The tetrahedron, of three dimensions, is bounded by four triangles, the two-dimensional analogues of the tetrahedra. The development of the triangle into

higher dimensions is extremely simple mathe-
matically, but it is quite as beautiful as the
development, of more complex forms. As the
tetrahedron is the first and simplest Platonic
solid, so the super-tetrahedron can be called
the first four-dimensional "platonic" solid.
The simplest form can bring the mind into
touch with higher space and so, for those who
regard the form as a means and not an end, it
is not necessary to go beyond the simplest
except as a help in visualizing simple forms.

We will now study in greater detail the
five-dimensional analogue of the cube and
tesseract, Fig. 5. I am not going to rely,
however, upon the diagram. The reader
should consult and try to make something of
it, but if he follows closely the following
description, building up in his mind the com-
ponent parts, trying at the same time to
vitalise them with the space of their own
dimensions, his efforts should be fruitful.

Visualize the cube, Fig. 6 the embodiment
of three-dimensional space showing at all
corners the three axes that define the limitations of the physical universe, realizing that
the superficies that bound the cube are differnt

Fig. 5

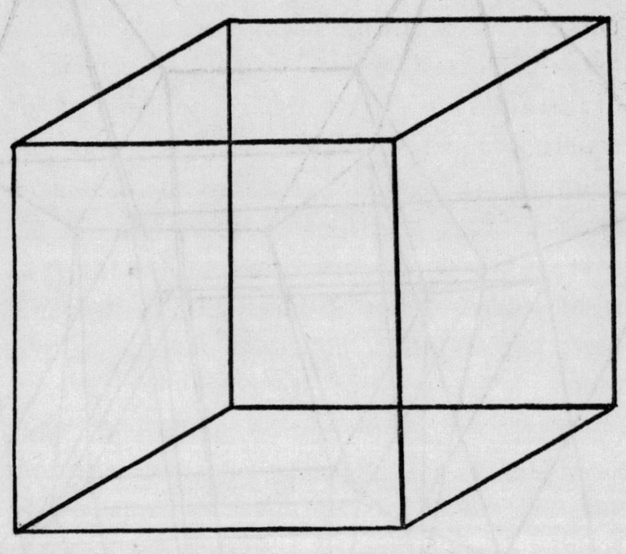

Fig. 6

in spatial nature from that of the cube: then project from each of the six squares a cube into the fourth dimension, so that the cubes projected from two adjoining squares, squares having a line in common, contact one another by a square that is formed by the extension of that line into the fourth dimension. The six squares, one from each projected cube and furthest from the primary cube, form another cube. The total of eight cubes enclose the tesseract, Fig. 2. Between these cubes is a portion of four-dimensional space, just as between the six squares of a cube is a portion of three-dimensional space. The cubes of the tesseract meet at their squares, and yet maintain right-angle relations towards each other because of the extra dimension. Each cube, however, has one other cube it is not at right angles to but is parallel to, in the same way that opposite squares of a cube do not touch each other but are parallel with each other. In four-dimensional space two cubes can be apart yet completely parallel with one another. To put it another way:—The volume of any one of the eight cubes is at right angles to all the others but one, and this one it is parallel to, although not occupying the same position in space. This is not necessary in a four-dimensional space, but such a parallelism is impossible between two objects in physical space. The nearest we can ever get to such a parallelism is by saying that an object is parallel with itself.

From each of the eight cubes enclosing the tesseract extends a tesseract into the fifth dimension. The outermost cubes of the tesseract form the eight boundaries of another tesseract, making a total of ten tesseracts meeting and fitting into one another so as to completely enclose a portion of five-dimensional space. The details of this figure (Fig. 5) can be visualized and an attempt made to get them into their true positions. Complete success is not to be expected for the object of this exercise is to make it easier to visualize a four-dimensional figure. However determined one may be in attempting to imagine a five-dimensional figure it is likely it will evade one, in its totality, for quite a while. The value of this exercise lies rather in the possibility that, as the mind relaxes from its efforts, a four-dimensional figure could much more easily enter the mind.

By the term ' mind ' I do not mean the brain. The brain is physical and three-dimensional. The mind, which finds expression through the brain, is not limited to three dimensions. Therefore, when a four-dimensional shape is visualized, the brain becomes quiescent, and subtler matter than the physical becomes the field of mental activity. It is probable that mental activity never does take place in the brain, but only in space contiguous to it. In the evolution of the human race the development, so far, has been within three-dimensional limitations. In the course of time humanity may develop four-dimensionally and become aware of a more spacious environment than it does at present.

In concluding this part I would like to briefly describe with the aid of Fig. 7, a seven dimensional shape, the simplest regular " solid " in seven-dimensional space. The diagram appears complicated for the simple reason that it is a drawing in two dimensions of a figure having four more dimensions than the shapes generally drawn on paper. The diagrams, Fig. 3 and Fig. 4 illustrate the analogous figures in three and four dimensions of this seven-dimensional figure. Just as at each corner of the tetrahedron its three dimensions are indicated by three lines meeting there so, at every corner of the seven-dimensional figure, its space is indicated by seven lines meeting there. In the diagram of the seven-diamensional form, apart from lines and triangles, there is, first, the base tetrahedron, then another four tetrahedra, all five being the boundary of the four-dimensional

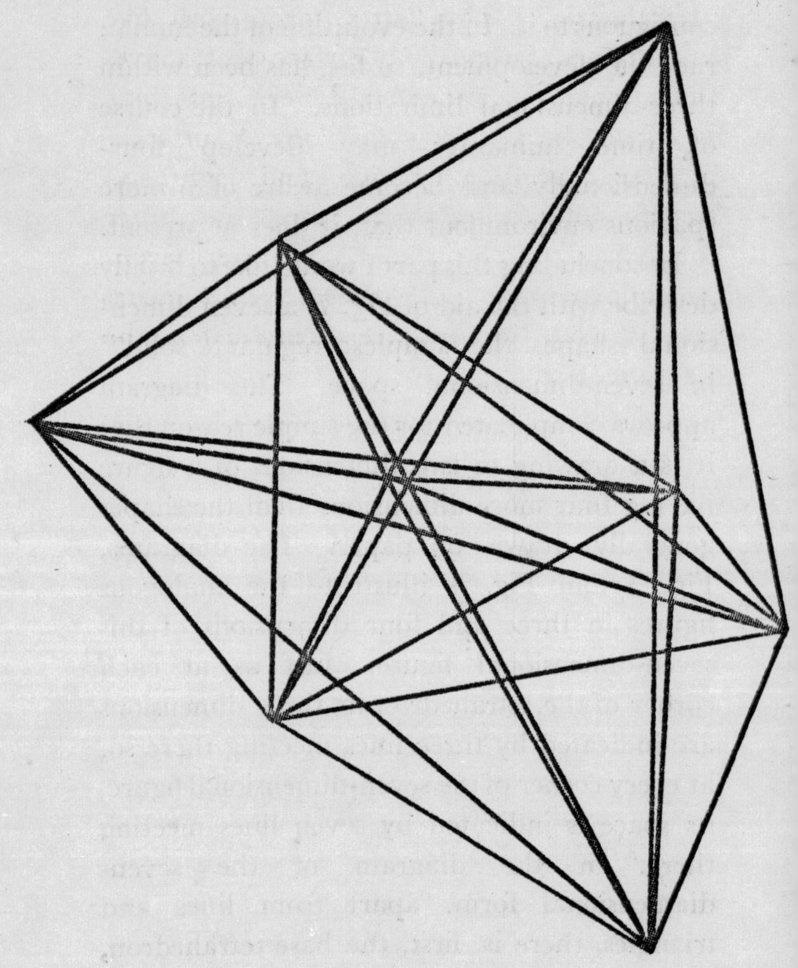

Fig. 7

" tetrahedra ". This latter form, with five similar ones, forms the " surface " of a five-dimensional " tetrahedra ". Seven of these five-dimensional forms are the " surface " of a six-dimensional shape, and eight six-dimensional " tetrahedra " are the outer boundaries or " surface " of the seven-dimensional form. All these details, apart from spatial content, are contained in the diagram, Fig. 7.

CHAPTER FIVE

PHILOSOPHICAL INTERLUDE

THE understanding of the fourth dimension, while it dissolves an old horizon and leaves a wider one, does not bring us to the fundamental condition which is the goal of philosophy. The mind of the true philosopher is set on the eternal, the infinite, and not on things as they appear to the senses and, just as three dimensions is not so much a property of matter as the way in which we look at it, so is it with the fourth dimension. We speak of three-dimensional space, and other spaces of more or less dimensions, but space has really no dimension. When we speak in this way what we really mean is a condition of consciousness limited to a perception of only three, or more and less, dimensional objects. It is the representations of the senses that makes us classify the universe in terms of dimensions.

The usual conception of the fourth dimension is, as I have already stated, of a direction at right angles to the three angles of the physical world. All the objects of this world have the quality of three-dimensionality. Perhaps, in the light of the argument now to be developed, it would be better to say that the space sense of human beings is, at present, capable of apprehending only three aspects of matter. By space sense I mean something different from the physical senses: the space sense, indeed, is something that evolves the ordinary senses. Later on we will see that this space sense is really nothing less than the cosmic working of consciousness. needing no organ in particular for it is that primordial sense of awareness that has existed since the dawn of manifestation.

To take again a simple object, a book: its three axes are these, one running its length, another across it, and the third from the front to the back cover. These three directions determine the space of the book and, if they were extended indefinitely, they would define the fields of all the stellar systems of the physical universe, subject of course to the spatial implications of a curved universe, computed by Dr. Edwin Hubble of Mt. Wilson Observatory to have a circumference of over two hundred billion light years. All the innumerable transformations of matter and intricacies of movement that we witness, for all their variety, are confined within certain definite and easily understandable limits, the three co-ordinates of geometry.

Another idea I would like to present is, that space is not, if at all, entirely an external thing but is what can be called a function of consciousness. If space was external to us, that is, independent of consciousness in the same way as the forms about us are, it would need to have a form, otherwise it could not exist. We say that we can see space but what we really see are objects in space. Space devoid of objects is inconceivable to us since it can only be conceived in our minds as nothingness or infinity. Space is infinite. When I speak of the infinity of space I do not mean, looking for the present at space as if it were an external condition, that it extends for ever in only three dimensions, meeting for us in this physical globe. I mean an absolute infinity, not in three but in all dimensions. We must accept the axiom that space has no form. That being so it cannot be limited by dimensions, for dimension is form. Space having no form it follows therefore, that as it is infinite, an object of any number of dimensions is possible in space. That conclusion seems inevitable. An object with any number of axes, at right angles to each other, is possible in space, its possibilities in this way are unlimited.

At first glance this question of whether space belongs to the outer world, or is a part of consciousness, is purely theoretical since there appears to be no solution to the problem. But if there is a space sense it follows then that if, by some process, we can enlarge this sense, then the objective world would take on larger horizons. The very existence of a sense makes the existence of a world of perception a "sine qua non." The senses we have today are the result of evolutionary processes but while there has been an evolution of specific organs, the space sense has existed since the beginning of things. Just as in material manifestations there is a unifying law so, using the specialised sense organs of our bodies, a fundamental sense has gazed out on the world, and drawn the drama of life into touch with its soul, the eternal life. This fundamental sense is the space sense. Through the ages there has been a constant inter-action between the outer and inner, the form and the life, through the space sense, and this sense belongs no more to the form than to the life side; therefore, while in the past we may have been compelled through ignorance to allow the sense organs to be evolved by the form side, there is no reason why the space sense should not be developed from within.

The question now to be gone into more fully is "What is Space?"

In beginning of this inquiry we are forced into several conclusions from which there is no escape, and therefore any philosophy that disputes them is at least that much false. The first axiom we are compelled to frame is, that the universe has always been. The second, that in manifestation we have two factors, life and form, force and matter, and the relation between them.

We have then two factors and their relation to each other, but what is this relation? It cannot be merely a figure of speech, an abstraction; it must have just as real an existence as life or matter. When we go more deeply into what we term the abstract, and the concrete, we find that the abstract is more real than the concrete simply because the former has an impersonal and therefore eternal life, whereas the latter has only a transitory one.

This relationship has always existed and is the means by which life contacts matter. It can be shown that matter in itself is propertyless, and similarly so with the life side. In fact they do not exist apart from one another. It therefore follows that all the properties that we assign to matter do not belong to it any more than to its partner, but that these properties are really the relation between them. Since there is only one relation, and there appear to be many properties of matter, how can this be so? The solution will be found in that all these properties or laws of matter are really only differentiations of the one principle, and that finally, just as various substances have a common atomic basis, so can we resolve all these diverse manifestations back to a common source, the relationship between matter and life. This relationship is consciousness. It therefore follows that since matter and life are propertyless in themselves, then time and space are part of consciousness and that we can equally well say that the relation between matter and life is time and space. In this primary conception of things we have the first conception of space. Spirit we can represent by a point, matter by another point. The relation between them is a line, the simplest of all dimensions, one dimension. Space, it can be seen here, is the means by which life contacts matter. It is consciousness.

If we go further into the question of what space is, we see that we are never conscious of space at all. We are conscious only of objects and that they are separate. This does not constitute space or rather is not space, for space is not constituted of anything, it is unity. We might even say that what we see is three-dimensional space, that we are conscious of three axes of a greater space. That would be equally erroneous so far as space is concerned. Space has no limitations. Space is not even the ether, that almost impalpable substance that extends through apparent space.

To repeat, space is a part of the conscious-ness and, as such, capable of infinite develop-ment. That is the practical issue of this argument, that life being logical and infinite in every way, a matter of law, and the space sense the means by which we come into contact with things, then there must be some process by which the space sense can be educated, so as to bring within its range secrets at present with-held from us only because we will not look. We are the victims of the objective world, accepting an illusion as an unescapable fact.

The reasoning I have so imperfectly put forth, but which I hope to improve upon another time, shows that it is impossible that matter can be limited to three dimensions and that therefore the principle of the geometers that " space has only three dimensions " is wrong, because space is unlimited. Kant says that this proposition of the geometers cannot be an empirical one nor a conclusion from an empirical judgment, but he is mistaken, for the judgment is derived from experience, and is not *a priori*.

Although I did not intend to touch on more than the philosophic aspect opened up by the problem of the fourth dimension yet, having demonstrated more or less the impossibility of the consciousness being limited to three dimensions, I feel it necessary to point the way by which an actual realisation of this truth can be obtained. This process by which first the mind, and then the waking consciousness, is brought into contact with the higher dimension utilises the imagination in building four-dimensional forms. The imagination working in this way is like a wedge, inexorably compelling the way to open before it. The fact that the mind can see four-dimensional figures, infers an exterior condition of four-dimensions, just as the existence of a book infers the continuation of its dimensions for infinity, embracing the whole of the cosmic physical plane. This higher dimensional world bears the same relation to the physical world as a sphere does to a circle. Thus, beginning with geometry, it is possible for us to pass into a greater life.

At times when one looks through philosophic eyes at the world, it seems to become more a phantasm than a real pulsating world, the home of many incarnations, especially when one feels compelled to accept the verdict of the pure reason, sealed with the approval of the intuition, that the ultimate things are unknowable, and that we must go on for ever ignorant of the first Cause, even though we reach the heights of gods. But, after a while one sees that what appear phantasms are phantasms, and that the objects we know are but appearances that hide a more intricate, but equally unsubstantial form, but the discovery of this form is not the reward: it is knowing that the form is not the Self, the eternal Spirit, for while, as Hinton has it, " in the awakening light of this new apprehension, the flimsy world quivers and shakes, rigid solids flow and mingle, all our material limitations turn to graciousness," yet, in all this flux, the Self stands undisturbed looking out over a ceaselessly changing world, for " This is the eternal state, O Son of Pritha. Who, even at the death hour, is established therein, he goeth to the Nirvana of the Eternal."

CHAPTER SIX

PHILOSOPHICAL DEFINITIONS

THE domain of philosophy is at once both simple and grand. It is grand because of its universality, and simple because the distinguishing feature of all universal propositions is their freedom from complexity. No better definition of philosophy could there be than Pythagoras' " Knowledge of immaterial and eternal things ". Philosophy is concerned only with infinite things. Now and again a proposition is framed that seems philosophically sound and, so far as experience shows, unimpeachable, and it is generally accepted as an absolute truth when actually it is only a relative one.

We hear much nowadays, too much perhaps, of the scientific mind. There is a philosophic mind also, a mind cast in its peculiar mould. Science is concerned with changing things, philosophy with eternal things, and the test of the philosophic mind, before admitting anything into the immaterial temple of philosophy, is " Is it infinite "? While the philosophic mind finds its greatest assurance in its own conclusions despite the contradiction of empirical evidence, it nevertheless asserts that somewhere in the material universe there must be evidence supporting these conclusions, since, after all, the universe is only an expression of philosophic truths.

The philosophic test is " Is it infinite ", ? and so, remembering this, we can weigh the philosophic evidence for the existence of a fourth dimension in space. Although in the future, for the purposes of expediency, I shall attempt definitions of space, yet I have come to the conclusion that space is indefinable. Space has that absoluteness that places it beyond definition and yet makes it possible to define it in innumerable ways. No one definition can ever be complete, although, if it is true within its limitations, it will serve as well as any other definition to lead to deeper truths, or to the Final Truth.

It seems to me that, in the pursuit of space, the mind is ever confronted by matter: to look out over space is to find other worlds, to look into space is to find finer matter. To look into space, what is meant by that? So long as we think of space as a connection between us and the exterior world, so long will a great part of the true nature of space evade us. We must learn to look into ,space as we would look into a painting. Outwardly the painting is but a plane of colour, but it has a message for us. Outwardly space is but a field in which the universes move, but it is more than that. It also has a message. But we must look into it as we would look into a painting. By the aid of such simple things as a canvas and oils we can come into touch with something immeasurably greater than these things. With the aid of the simplest of forms we can also come into touch with a space immeasurably greater than our space, matter immeasurably subtler than physical matter.

My concern now is not, however, to show how to come into touch with this higher space, but to demonstrate its existence.

The proposition of space can be worded, somewhat as follows, " Space is infinite in every dimension." That is a proposition to which the philosophic mind can take no exception for it means that space extends to infinity in every dimension. What can be taken exception to, however, is a misinterpretation of the word " every " which is unconsciously translated to mean " three ". The proposition " Space is infinite in only three dimensions " (to add a word to emphasise the meaning) is philosophically unsound, and therefore untrue. The idea of finiteness is obtained purely from empirical sources, and philosophic truths are not based merely upon the evidence of the senses. There is this difference between relative and absolute—that is philosophic—truths: while the former are true in only one instance, the latter are always true.

The evidence denoted by the title of this essay could be very briefly set out as follows. Space is here treated objectively.

Proposition: Space is infinite in every dimension.

Proofs: There are two aspects contained in the proposition to be demonstrated: the infinity of space in each dimension, and the infinity of space dimensionally.

Proof I. If a particular space, i.e., of one, two, three etc., dimensions was limited in its extent, that limitation must be either material or non-material. Matter, however, cannot limit space, it occupies space, and to say that the limitation is not material is to say that it does not exist. The limitation of the extent of space is inconceivable because the existence of space is a necessity to the conception of a limitation, and therefore any limitation we conceive must be in space and not out of it. The conclusion then is that space is infinite in extent.

Proof II. If space is limited to three dimensions, that which limits it must be either outside or within the three dimensions. It cannot, however, be within, for we would then have the anomaly of a limiting thing being the limited thing. As shown in Proof I three-dimensional space is infinite in extent, but, even if we were to allow that a limitation could exist in three dimensions, it could only be a limitation of the extent of three-dimensional space, and not that which limits space to three dimensions. The limitation, therefore, must be outside three dimensions. As this limitation must occupy space to be outside three dimensions, it must be in a different kind of space, and differences in space lie only in differences in number of dimensions. The simplest space not included in three-dimensional space is a four-dimensional space. Therefore the limitation of three dimensions must be the fourth dimension. But the fourth dimension must be limited also, and similarly, so with that which limits the fourth dimension, and so on *ad infinitum*. Therefore space is unlimited dimensionally.

Corollaries: A thing cannot be limited without being limited by something (of necessity material), and therefore to grant that there is a restriction and at the same time to deny a restrictive agent is to set up a contradiction: to admit that the visible world is limited to three dimensions, and to deny the existence of that which limits it (of necessity the fourth dimension) is to create the same contradiction. But to admit the existence of the fourth dimension, and to deny the existence of the fifth is to occupy, if possible, an even more untenable position.

Since there cannot be space where there is no matter, to say that space is infinite in dimensions is to say that matter is infinite in dimensions. Just as space cannot in any way be limited since all limitations occupy space, so matter also is unlimited since all limitations are material. Thus, with the same breath that it is stated that matter is limited, it is asserted that matter transcends limitation. Matter is both slave and master.

It may be asserted—it can never be argued logically—that space and matter, for some reason that will never be known, have been cast permanently in three dimensions only. It may be contended that no other form of space and matter is possible. An elementary knowledge of the theory of the fourth dimension would show on what thin ice such assertions as these find support. There can be no disputing that the fourth dimension is theoretically possible, for it is within the power of the mind to attain to a knowledge of four-dimensional forms and movements that falls little short of the real thing. There are perhaps, a few minds that have perceived the fourth dimension in its fulness, but even to such as these how to describe this fulness is a problem that will always remain a problem. It is something to be experienced, not described, and in this experiencing all three-dimensional limitations drop away from the mind. It is for no one to define limits blindly. I say blindly, for to earnestly seek limits and define them is to pass beyond them. Limitations are relative and not absolute. Such a proposition as " Space has only three dimensions " can become a superstition.

In presenting the preceding argument briefly there is much that needs elaborating, and indeed, at first sight, it seemed almost hopeless attempting to formulate in so brief a form such an extensive argument, but for the sake of indicating my main contention that the fourth dimension is a fact in nature and therefore demonstrable philosophically, I have essayed such a demonstration.

CHAPTER SEVEN

IMMORTALITY AND THE FOURTH DIMENSION

IT may seem paradoxical to bring together two ideas that in some ways appear mutually exclusive. The very word immortality exhales the atmosphere of the infinite, while the fourth dimension suggests the finite. But while the four-dimensional state, regarded only as a world of larger consciousness and activity than the physical world, may not have the absolute significance we attach to the idea of immortality, in another sense it bears the mark of the eternal for, since most of us, in the waking consciousness, are limited to the physical dimensions of space, the fourth dimension is symbolical for us of that mysterious unknown region of consciousness which lies, which always lies, just beyond the boundaries of our normal experience. Besides the particular meanings it carries, in the Relativity Theory, it also has this universal character—the fourth dimension, as the next expansion of consciousness to be experienced by humanity, symbolises for us the undiscovered regions of the human spirit, the strange country that lies over the next hill.

But it symbolises not only the next step for us in space; the fourth dimension, by virtue of its character of being so different from anything we know here on earth, is the symbol of that which is also utterly different from this physical universe of relativity, that timeless and spaceless Reality which we call the Absolute. The experience of this Absolute is the only genuine attainment of immortality, and my intention is to develop the idea that we are here and now essentially immortal, and that the realisation of our immortal condition is possible here and now, if we but face the most elementary facts of our being.

What is it, then, that appears the most fundamental thing in our consciousness? Or if we prefer the formulation, what is the most fundamental thing in the world about us? If so, are we limited to two words, time and space? All objects occupy space and move in time, or to put it another way, space and time are of the very nature of the relative consciousness, and therefore all that appears in that consciousness takes on the qualities of form and change.

Here, then is the key to Immortality. We must understand the real nature of space and time, and discover their eternal significance. We must conquer the world of relativity to experience the Absolute. Immortality is freedom from all the limitations of that which we call the material world, it is the attainment of the state of change-lessness where the consciousness being universal, no sense of past and future, near and far, arises in it because consciousness touched time and space at every point. This is the ultimate mystical experience in which the mystic finds his heart to be the universe.

Regarded from the philosophical viewpoint, there is only one space—Absolute Space, any relative space, such as the field of our physical activities, being but a creation of the limited individual consciousness. Each creation, or realization in time and space of Eternal

Reality is unique, for no two individuals can occupy the same position in time and space with regard to a particular event. It seems obvious that two persons cannot occupy precisely the same position in space, but it may be argued that they can occupy the same position in time with regard to a particular event. It can be demonstrated, however, that time is but a dimension of space experienced in a certain way, and that the general conception of the past as being eternally lost and the future yet to have existence is due to an illusion. Relative space is a creation of the limited consciousness, and gives the impression of being infinite, because of what might be called the ' pressure ' of the Absolute on the separated consciousness; the sense of infinity is due to the mind giving to the finite universe it creates the nature of the uncreated universe.

This world of the senses, of the mind, is definitely finite, and though we press further and further into the depths of space we only establish more than ever the fact of the finiteness of the visible universe, the universe of relativity; we pass from one finiteness to a relatively greater finiteness. There is no limit to this passing on to larger and still larger horizons by the mind, for the relative universe can never exhaust the possibilities of the Absolute. We must, however, draw a distinction between the universe as it really is, and as we must know it through the senses and the mind. The real universe is without spatial limitation, the universe of science, of the senses, and the mind is always limited in extent. There is also another limitation determining events in a relative universe, the number of its dimensions.

A term sometimes used in describing Eternal or Absolute Existence is the Immeasurable, because all measurements, largeness and smallness, are entirely relative and can have no meaning in that mystery to the finite mind, Absolute Space. But we could not conceive a physical universe, a material, a measurable universe, but for that property of relative space which we define as its dimensions. Our physical space has dimensions to the number of three, disregarding for present purposes the dimension of time; our physical consciousness is three-dimensional. This geometrically stated means that three straight lines at right angles to each other completely define space relationships in the whole physical universe. The dimensions or co-ordinates of a cube are the reference lines of this universe, a universe which, though telescopic power be increased a millionfold, can never be plumbed. Can this universe then, seeing there is no end to its expansion from finiteness to greater finiteness, be the scene of Immortal Life which also has no end?

No! For even though we were to grant the endlessness of space in the usual sense, we see it is finite in another sense. It has only three dimensions. The immortal state is unlimited, therefore it must be infinitely-dimensioned, or undimensioned; convertible terms, just as when we say a universe is infinite in size we mean it has no size since it is immeasurable. Size is entirely relative, and any object considered in itself is neither large nor small. Eternal Existence can be thought of somewhat in this way, but with a difference. The Absolute is without size, not because it is isolated from everything else, but because nothing else exists to isolate it from. What in the relative consciousness appears as measurable, in the Absolute has actually no size, since the Absolute, of its very nature, contains or rather is, no standard of comparison. Our experience of this physical universe is a realization in three dimensions of that undimensioned or infinitely-dimensioned Reality, Absolute Space.

What, then has the fourth dimension, seeing it also is finite, to do with Immortality? Its supreme value is that, because of its nature of being geomertically greater than, and what is more important, spatially different from, the physical world, it awakens the intuition of space, of the real nature of space, leading the human spirit on to a final realization of its immortal condition. When the mind is aware of only one kind of space, has experienced form in only one set of dimensions, that of physical space, it accepts that limitation without questioning it, without even realizing it exists: but when another dimension is added to consciousness, when a higher space is experienced, then the mind wonders whether this extra dimension, conferring though it does greater powers on the mind, is not also a limitation of consciousness. Whereas before the intuition of space was awakened the dimensions of space were unconscious limitations, they now become conscious limitations.

They are tangibly felt as restrictions on consciousness, on the mind at first, later on as determining the fields in which still higher faculties manifest. So it is that into the mind just awakening to the real nature of space there flashes an intuition that dimension means limitation, that in the attainment of immortality man transcends all limitations and enters into an experience of space as pure consciousness, having no limitations whatsoever. The value, then, of an inquiry into the nature of the fourth dimension is that it brings under critical examination a limitation that has so gently oppressed human consciousness as to have passed practically unnoticed and unfelt by mankind in general.

By presenting the fourth dimension purely as a speculation in geometry without insisting on any other kind of reality, mathematicians save themselves from the charge of heresy. But I would insist on the reality of the fourth dimension in consciousness, and as a world or universe having the same validity as the world

of our physical experience. The idea that
the objects about us are completely solid,
in the geometrical sense, and final in the
number of their dimensions, is an absurdity.
If it were not for the backing of higher dimensions the physical universe would be flimsier
than the frailest of tissue paper. The very
existence of this universe is dependent on the
fact that it is a facet of an Existence infinitely-
dimensioned.

A two-dimensional world is often imagined
as a vast superficies like the surface of a calm
ocean, with flat creatures of exceeding thinness,
moving on but never away from it. They
would be completely oblivious of the sky
above and the watery depths below. This is
a consistent illustration of the nature of a
two-dimensional world, for it shows how these
creatures, though unconscious of anything
beyond life on a surface, are nevertheless surrounded in directions beyond their possibility
of understanding (as two-dimensional beings)
by a universe immeasurably greater. Indeed
the very existence of their world is dependent
on the existence of ocean and sky. The
picture of surface beings oblivious of the space

above and below their plane of experience brings to mind the opening sentence of C. W. Leadbeater's book, 'The Astral Plane': "Though for the most part entirely unconscious of it, man passes the whole of his life in the midst of a vast and populous unseen world."

All this preamble to my main contention that immortality is ours here and now, and that we can realize that immortality, is but an emphasis of the fact that the absolute universe is a homogeneous existence of infinite dimensions, that we exist in this absolute universe but persist in looking at only a facet of it, a three-dimensional section of eternal being, and finally, that by understanding the nature of space limitations we can transcend them, we can experience space as pure consciousness.

If from the centre of our consciousness we extended indefinitely two lines at right angles, like a cross, and all the events we were aware of could be completely determined by reference to these two lines, or co-ordinates, our consciousness would be two-dimensional. If our experience of events in space were determined by reference to three lines at right angles crossing each other at the centre of our consciousness, that consciousness would be three-dimensional. But if four lines at right angles completely defined our objective experience, then should we be conscious of a world in comparison with which the physical universe is but a shadow world. Physical death would have another meaning, since it requires four-space co-ordinates for its determination as an event in the relative world.

However, the changing from one state of consciousness to another, in other words, human survival, does not meet the requirements of the definition of Immortal Life, for the essence of that condition, or rather, unconditioned state, is changelessness. It is true that we have a seeming immortality in the fact of the continuity of consciousness, but the continuity is of a limited consciousness. To realize our immortality we must experience a state untouched by any limitation, we must 'enter' into a universe of pure consciousness, undimensioned because infinitely dimensioned. How are we to experience this immortal state? How are we to become one with the Absolute?

We have seen that two lines meeting in a point are the reference lines of a two-dimensional consciousness, three lines meeting in a point the reference lines of physical consciousness, and four lines the co-ordinates of a four-dimensional consciousness. Although these co-ordinates vary in number from each state of consciousness, there is one thing all sets of co-ordinates have in common, the point of meeting place of the lines. If this point is expanded in two dimensions it is seen as a circle, if in three dimensions as a sphere, and if expanded in four dimensions it becomes a four dimensional globe, a form only superficially describable to physical consciousness. What I wish to stress, however, is that the point is the meeting place of the dimensions, not only of two, three or four, but of infinite dimensions, and that every point in space is the meeting place of infinite dimensions. The Absolute then is something to be experienced at and in every point of the universe. The dimensions of infinity meet in a point, and that point for the individual is the centre of his consciousness. That point is the Absolute. The point has no magnitude, but to have no magnitude does not mean non-existence any more than Nirvana means annihilation. The point is Immeasurable Being. We thus find that this definition of a point is precisely the same as that of Eternal Existence, the state of Immortality, which means they are identical. The mind, in its time-and-space arrogance, may object: " But the point is infinitely small and the Absolute immeasurably large." The mind cannot understand the paradox of that which is without dimension being equal to the infinitely-dimensioned, since it is inherently incapable of knowing Ultimate Truth or Reality.

The nature of Consciousness is such that no division can take place in it; it is a unity, the division into relative states of dimensioned consciousness being an illusion we are not inexorably compelled to accept. There is only one consciousness, and its centre, which is, relatively speaking, everywhere, is the heart of each individual consciousness.

The individual consciousness is a point of infinite dimensions, pure space, the Immeasurable. It is because we are this universal consciousness, immortality is for us. In all of us there is at least a dim apprehension of this fact. What we have to do is to make this faint realization of our immortality blossom into what appears to be the relative universe, when occurs that which crowns our conscious immortality. The perception of the universe, as a field of relativity, dissolves into a realization of it as Absolute Being. Life, consciousness, matter, are merged in one Unconditioned Existence. These three aspects of the Absolute appear in the Christian religion as Father, Son and Holy Ghost. The Father is Life, the Son Universal Consciousness or Pure Space, and the Holy Ghost dimensions or relative space.

Our special consideration now is the Second Person of the Trinity. This is Divine Love crucified, as we say, in matter, and appearing in the human spirit as universal love, the Christ-consciousness. Is not this aspect similar to Pure Space or Pure Consciousness, in contact at every point with the whole universe? And the cross on which this universal consciousness is crucified is the cross of finite dimensions passing through every point of the relative universe. The Christ Love of the Christian and the Pure Space of metaphysics are identical, and the philosopher who has passed from speculation to experience of Reality finds his whole being merged with that of the mystic, who has found his Peace, in that ineffable Existence variously called the Supreme, God, and the Immortal State.

This, then is how the experience of the Fourth Dimension sheds light on the nature of Immortality, how the enlargement of the relative consciousness can mean the experience of Absolute Consciousness. We discover that one thing remains constant in our experience of three and four-dimensional states of consciousness, the centre of consciousness, that inner integrity which at different levels of manifestation is called soul, ego, Monad, Logos. From birth to death our bodies grow, mature, and decay, but we, the Immortal Centre of our bodies, our environment, our universe, grow not; neither are we subject to birth and death. Such events are partial glimpses of Reality framed on some of the infinite dimensions of our being, events measured along three co-ordinates instead of

being " related " to Eternal Space. We are
mortal, or think we are mortal, because we
identify ourselves with a limited universe
instead of living in that point sometimes called
the Inner Self, but which is neither inner nor
outer since we are that Self, the Immortal
Centre of life, timeless and without position
save when related by the mind to its self-
created universe. And when we live in that
timeless Centre, which is our real existence,
we know that for us has been no age-long
pilgrimage, for us there has not been, in the
words of Longfellow,

   ' All the aching heart, the restless unsatisfied
     longing,
   All the dull deep pain, and constant anguish
     of patience,'

for the dimensions of space and time restrict
alone the body born in time. The soul,
though seemingly immersed in mortal things,
remains where neither sin nor interdict of
man can darken its bright aureole, nor space
and time enmesh its mighty wings.

SONNETS OF SPACE AND TIME

1

Upon a geometric base whose three,
So few and yet sublime, co-ordinates
Define the field where spin the sister Fates
The warp and woof of human destiny,
I see uprise a shape so strange to me,
A being born to haunt time's narrow straits,
And so inevitably my mind restates
In wider terms its immortality.
And when stern death commands my body's
    dust
To mingle with the dust of finite stars
My soul, uprising from the pulseless clay,
Will spread its pinions heavy with the rust
Of earth and, passing through the three-fold
    bars,
Pursue again its transcendental way.

2

When first my mind confronted time and space
And grappled with antiquity, a sense
Of vast remoteness chilled such eloquence
As stirs within the heart when face to face
With unconditioned forms of change and place.
I thought of a world without circumference,
Intensified by time's omniscience,
Too wide for human reason to embrace.

Until to-night, conversing with the stars,
I see their orbits blossom into curves
Along whose spiral paths no feet have trod;
And as I gaze no sound nor movement mars
The massive tapestry of cosmic nerves,
For time has fled and Space is god.

3

How vast and still is this Einsteinian world
That slowly breaks upon my steadfast gaze.
The stars, before pursuing devious ways,
Now merge in paths along which once they
    hurled
Till all I see are helices upcurled

From awful distances of bygone days
To heights of unborn years.   In thrilled amaze
I watch a universe where time is furled

In coils of manifold intricacy.
O Space! what mystery now reveals your
        wonder,
And makes of form a phantom episode?
For curves dissolve into the poetry
Within my heart to lose their spiral splendour
Of shape, and I of time and place am God.

4

Dimension on dimension fades into
The centre of my being, first the three
Of space and one of time, the empery
Of mortal man, then worlds beyond earth's woe
Though not beyond extension or time's flow,
Where space and time approach infinity.
Of that immortal life there is for me
No certainty as yet, but this I know:

The prison walls of time and space restrict
Alone the body born in time.   The soul
Though seemingly immersed in mortal things,
Remains where neither sin nor interdict

Of man can darken its bright aureole,
Nor space and time enmesh its mighty wings.

5

What intricate designs are deftly etched,
Within the void of space by satellites
And planets as they shed their days and nights
Along elliptic paths, what rhythm sketched
In curves across immensities outstretched
By streaming groups of stars. Such grace invites
The mind to further contemplate the rites
Of ever-restless globes until, bewitched

By visions of bright galaxies, it sees
The myriad motions of the heavens merge
Into a universal drift through time
That carries all, like some immortal breeze,
With uniform velocity from verge
To infinite verge of this celestial clime.

6

The universe, mediaeval priests proclaim,
Is but a finite dome whose outer space
Beyond the roof of stars is heaven, whose base,

The earth, conceals the purgatorial flame.
Then speaks a man, Copernicus by name:-
The stars and suns are urged with infinite grace
To move eternally from place to place
And earth, revolving, cloaks no secret shame.

And now a mind of equal magnitude
Appears, to coax a deeper truth from space.
Not heaven and hell confine its full extension,
Nor that dim region where abysses brood
Through barren days. Upon a timeless base
Space broadens from dimension to dimension.

7

The harmony of satellites and stars
Has been established and maintained they say
By gravitation constantly at play
Forming a network of invisible bars,
That sweep across the sky like scimitars
Between each body in this vast array,
As galaxies and systems cleave their way
According to celestial calendars.

But this say I:—no force that straightly acts
Along Euclidian lines preserves the distances

Of spinning globes in three-dimensional space;
The universe like cubes in tesseracts,
Is but a facet of sublime existences
Whose structure no geometry can trace.